THE TWELVE DAYS
OF
SPRINGTIME

A School Counting Book

by Deborah Lee Rose

illustrated by Carey Armstrong-Ellis

Abrams Books for Young Readers, New York

1 On the first day of springtime,
my teacher gave to me . . .

Life
Cycle
of the
Monarch

egg

caterpillar

butterfly

chrysalis

Happy spring!

12

riding jacket

. . . a garden to water carefully.

2 On the second day of springtime,
my teacher gave to me
TWO turtle ponds
and a garden to water carefully.

3 On the third day of springtime,
my teacher gave to me
THREE seedlings,
two turtle ponds,
and a garden to water carefully.

On the blackboard:

Hymenoptera

Lepidoptera

riding boots

Helicoptera

I am not an insect!

4 On the fourth day of springtime,
my teacher gave to me
FOUR ladybugs,
three seedlings,
two turtle ponds,
and a garden to water carefully.

5 On the fifth day of springtime,
my teacher gave to me
FIVE gold stars,
four ladybugs,
three seedlings,
two turtle ponds,
and a garden to water carefully.

On the sixth day of springtime,
my teacher gave to me
SIX signs for reading,
five gold stars,
four ladybugs,
three seedlings,
two turtle ponds,
and a garden to water carefully.

On the seventh day of springtime,
my teacher gave to me
SEVEN notes for singing,
six signs for reading,
five gold stars,
four ladybugs,
three seedlings,
two turtle ponds,
and a garden to water carefully.

8

On the eighth day of springtime,
my teacher gave to me
EIGHT wings for wearing,
seven notes for singing,
six signs for reading,
five gold stars,
four ladybugs,
three seedlings,
two turtle ponds,
and a garden to water carefully.

9 On the ninth day of springtime,
my teacher gave to me
NINE ducks for drawing,
eight wings for wearing,
seven notes for singing,
six signs for reading,
five gold stars,
four ladybugs,
three seedlings,
two turtle ponds,
and a garden to water carefully.

10

On the tenth day of springtime,
my teacher gave to me
TEN words for rhyming,
nine ducks for drawing,
eight wings for wearing,
seven notes for singing,
six signs for reading,
five gold stars,
four ladybugs,
three seedlings,
two turtle ponds,
and a garden to water carefully.

Tomorro
Nature
walk!

HORSE
of course

11 On the eleventh day of springtime,
my teacher gave to me
ELEVEN stones for stepping,
ten words for rhyming,
nine ducks for drawing,
eight wings for wearing,
seven notes for singing,
six signs for reading,
five gold stars,
four ladybugs,
three seedlings,
two turtle ponds,
and a garden to water carefully.

12

On the twelfth day of springtime,
my teacher gave to me
TWELVE flags for flapping,
eleven stones for stepping,
ten words for rhyming,
nine ducks for drawing,
eight wings for wearing,
seven notes for singing,
six signs for reading . . .

. . . five gold stars,
four ladybugs,
three seedlings,
two turtle ponds . . .

. . . and a garden to water carefully.

For my friends, who are the *blooms* and *butterflies* in my garden. —D.L.R.

To the Booksters, one and all, for their advice, support, and friendship,
and to Deb for keeping me *busy* all these years! —C.A.-E.

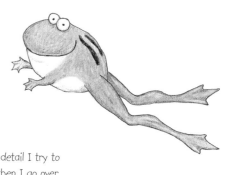

Artist's Note:
After enlarging my *sketches*, I transfer them onto hot press watercolor paper, which has a smooth surface necessary for all the detail I try to fit into my pictures. I then outline the major figures in ink with a technical drawing pen. I use gouache to paint in the colors, and then I go over everything with colored pencil to add detail and shading. Frequently, I go back after that with a teeny-weeny brush to add little things like hairs and insect legs. My must-haves? An electric pencil sharpener, good music, and strong magnifying glasses!

The TWELVE flags for flapping are, from left to right and top to bottom: Japan, Liechtenstein, United States, Mexico, China, Brazil, Ghana, rainbow peace flag, automobile-racing flag, United Kingdom, Canada, Papua New Guinea.

The rainbow peace flag was first used in Italy in 1961 and is often seen with the Italian word for "peace"—*pace*—written on it.
The black-and-white checkered flag is used in automobile racing to mark the end of a race.

Library of Congress Cataloging-in-Publication Data

Rose, Deborah Lee.
   The twelve days of springtime : a school counting book / by Deborah Lee Rose ; illustrated by Carey Armstrong-Ellis.
      p. cm.
   ISBN 978-0-8109-8330-4 (Harry N. Abrams)
   1. Counting—Juvenile literature. 2. Counting—Juvenile poetry. 3. Spring—Juvenile literature. I. Armstrong-Ellis, Carey. II. Title.
   QA113.R672 2009
   513.2'11—dc22

                              2008024358

Text copyright © 2009 Deborah Lee Rose
Illustrations copyright © 2009 Carey Armstrong-Ellis
Book design by Vivian Kimball

Abrams Books for Young Readers are available at special discounts when purchased in quantity for premiums and promotions as well as fundraising or educational use. Special editions can also be created to specification. For details, contact specialmarkets@hnabooks.com or the address below.

Printed and bound in China
10 9 8 7 6 5 4 3 2 1

HNA ▮▯▯▮▮ 115 West 18th Street
harry n. abrams, inc. New York, NY 10011
a subsidiary of La Martinière Groupe   www.hnabooks.com